D1093090

An Unlucky Miss!

THE
GOLDEN BUDGET
FOR BOYS

BLACKIE & SON LIMITED
LONDON AND GLASGOW

BLACKIE & SON LIMITED
  50 Old Bailey, London
  17 Stanhope Street, Glasgow

BLACKIE & SON (INDIA) LIMITED
  Warwick House, Fort Street, Bombay

BLACKIE & SON (CANADA) LIMITED
  Toronto

Printed in Great Britain by Blackie & Son, Ltd., Glasgow

CONTENTS

A FRIEND IN NEED

I

Barry Crisp, helpless with a broken leg on his cot in the palm-leaf shack heard steps race across the clearing. Then in rushed his brother Jim, and the glow on his face told Barry the news without need for words.

" You've got it, Jim?" he asked sharply.

" I've got it, Barry—got it at last. Look at this."

He handed the other a lump about the size of two fists. It was greyish in colour, very heavy and, faint as the light was, there was enough to see the thin yellow lines that veined it. Barry's eyes widened.

" Gosh, Jim, it's nearly one-fifth gold. There—there can't be much of this."

" There's a vein a foot wide and I don't yet know how long." Jim's voice rang a triumph. " Barry, we've got it at last. Our fortunes are made. As soon as your leg's well we'll load up the batelone and go off down the river with enough gold to keep us for the rest of our lives." Barry did not speak. He was gazing at the lump of ore.

A deep purring broke the silence and into the hut

came a beast like a giant cat. From his whiskers to the end of his tail he was nine feet of silky perfection, his tawny coat covering muscles like tempered steel. Jim rubbed the puma's great head and its purring bubbled like a giant kettle.

" Pintado knows all about it. He's as pleased as we are, Barry." Barry stretched out a thin hand and stroked the magnificent beast.

" I'm glad he's with you, Jim," he said significantly.

" Why?"

" Because of Parral." Jim's lip curled.

" That yellow pig. I'm not afraid of him."

" But you ought to be afraid of him," Barry's voice was urgent. " He's deadly dangerous. Remember he claims to own this land and the minerals in it."

" And you and I know he does nothing of the sort," returned Jim curtly. " El Sertão is all Government land and Luis Parral has no claim to anything beyond his homestead."

" He'd sell his soul for that gold," Barry insisted. " There's no trick too dirty for that yellow fiend. Tell me, where did you find the vein?"

" In the old workings up the hillside—above the place we first tried. It's all right. Parral knows nothing. Now I'm going to fix up some grub." He set to cooking and Barry watched him and wondered.

Jim was a marvel. He was as cool as though finding a fortune in gold was just an incident, and quite plainly he was not a bit scared of Parral. Barry was. He knew the cruel covetous mind of this half-bred Portuguese and Indian, and knew, too, that sooner or later, the man would come to know of their great find.

Here, in the wilds of the Brazilian forest, no law ran. He and Jim might be wiped out without the slightest fear of consequences. Parral might shoot them from ambush and then had only to dump their bodies in the river. The pirai would see to it that nothing was left.

Jim stayed with his brother the rest of the day. Only one bone of the leg was broken and that was mending nicely, yet for the time Barry was quite helpless. Soon after six the sun set and darkness shut down. A hot darkness full of the hum of insects, the splash of fish in the river and the weird cries of night birds in the jungle surrounding the clearing.

The brothers ate their supper. An omelette of turtles' eggs, pancakes made of maize flour and a pot of coffee. And while they ate they talked.

Pintado, lying flat on his side like a great cat, stirred and sat up. His green eyes shone like lamps.

" Someone coming," Barry whispered, and Jim, snatching up a gun, slipped silently out into the night. Quiet as he was, the intruder heard. Jim caught a glimpse of a dark form disappearing into the thick of the forest, there was a faint rustle, then all was quiet. Jim came back.

" Parral?" Barry asked.

" Very likely," said Jim briefly.

" Then he was listening."

" He's gone," said Jim. " Don't worry, Barry. Pintado will warn us if he comes again."

Jim refused to be worried and slept peacefully that night. He trusted to the panther. He himself had rescued it as a cub—found it abandoned and forlorn in a hole in the rock. What had happened to its mother he never knew, and the beast repaid him with a doglike devotion.

" Amigo del christiano," the Brazilians call this creature, that is, " The Christian's Friend ", and no other of the cat tribe is less cat-like in its nature.

At dawn Jim had breakfast ready and after making Barry comfortable, went away up the hillside. Pintado followed silently. He was rarely a dozen yards away from his master and Barry was comforted that his brother had such a guardian.

Seven hundred feet above the valley Jim came to the mouth of the old mine. Perhaps he was the first human to enter it for a thousand years, for the identity of those who had originally cut these great galleries into the heart of the hill was one of Brazil's many mysteries. He lit his lamp, picked up his tools and passed on into the cool darkness where the only sound was the drip of water from the rock roof.

The light was reflected from gleaming threads of gold and Jim swung his pickaxe and started work. A week, or at most a fortnight, and he would have enough of this rich ore to load the big batelone, then he and Barry would drift away down the river bound for San Lino where the big steamers call.

What ore! It was incredibly rich. Some of it was almost half gold. He hummed a little tune as he worked and never noticed that Pintado was uneasy. The great puma was standing up, looking towards the entrance. A growl rumbled in his deep throat.

Came a boom like distant gun-fire. The air quivered, the lantern light jumped. Jim leaped round, and as he did so there was a loud rumble of falling rock. He snatched up the lantern and ran to the mouth, only to find it completely blocked by broken masses of rock. Through the chinks came Parral's sneering voice.

" You and your cat. You can stay there and eat gold."

II

For a moment Jim stood, stunned by the shock. It needed but a single glance to see that it was impossible to get out. It would take a week to clear that mass of rock and he had no food, and light for perhaps four hours! No more, for he had meant to go back at mid-day to look after Barry.

Barry—fear for his brother gave Jim a worse shock than his own plight, for Barry, helpless, was at the mercy of this black-hearted brute.

Almost any man in Jim's place would have despaired, but Jim was not built that way, and as soon as the first numbing shock had passed he began to think of some way out of his terrible plight. The workings were of great extent, and it was just possible there was another way out. It was a slim chance, yet the only one. He did not know where to look for it, and the odds were strong that he might wander in this maze of subterranean galleries until he died. He had no food and all the gold in the mine would not buy him a mouthful.

But there was no use in thinking about that. He had to remember that every moment his oil was burning away. He must use every minute of light in the search.

Away he went, Pintado at his heels. It was something to have the company of this splendid beast. To a person alone in such a plight as Jim's madness comes.

Soon Jim found himself on unknown ground. The galleries were like a great maze but seemed all on one level. At last he found one that sloped steeply upwards. It led into a large square chamber with no outlet. Jim had to go all the way back.

Deeper in he discovered a square shaft leading down into black depths. This told him that there was a lower level but did not help him to reach it. He had no rope.

A FRIEND IN NEED

On he went again. There were miles of cuts and cross-cuts, and after a time Jim lost all sense of direction. He found himself in a passage half-choked with fallen rock. Pintado lagged behind. He did not like the place. Jim turned, and lucky for him that he did, for with a thunderous crash a couple of tons of stone smashed down just where he had been standing a moment earlier. In spite of himself he shivered at the narrowness of his escape.

The light grew dim, he looked at his lamp and realized that he had hardly any oil left. The thought of being left in the darkness sent a fresh shudder through him.

The light burned lower and lower. Jim began to hurry. It is fatal to hurry in a mine. He struck his head on a jag of rock projecting downwards from the roof and stumbled forward on his face, stunned.

When he came to he was in pitch darkness. Groping, he found his lantern, but it lay on its side and the last drop of oil had leaked out.

Jim struck a match and the glimmer was reflected in the green orbs of the puma.

" We're done for, old chap," said Jim with the quietness of despair. The great beast came close

Lost in a maze of rock!

and nuzzled him. Jim put an arm round the sinewy neck and dragged himself to his feet. His head ached sorely. He felt the puma drawing away. The creature wanted to move. With his hand on its neck and his head bowed, Jim followed.

Pintado went on steadily and, to his surprise, Jim found himself going up a steep slope. Pacing quietly, the tawny monster went on and on, and Jim wondered vaguely what was its goal. He had no hope that it could find a way out of this rock maze, yet it seemed better to keep moving than to lie still and die in the dark.

On and on. The slope seemed endless but at last the floor was level. What was more, the air which, below, had been thick and heavy, was now fresher. Jim stopped and struck another match. The small flame flickered in a current of air—which blew straight in his face. Yet the gallery was just like all the others through which he had passed.

The match went out and Pintado went on. Jim's heart was thumping. Hope had come back, for the current of air upon his face grew stronger.

It was not quite so dark. A greyness showed before his straining eyes. The puma's pace quickened, then suddenly Jim shouted, for a square patch of daylight showed in front. A minute later he plunged out into the light of the setting sun and dropped on a ledge dazzled and exhausted. Then he flung his arms round the puma's neck.

" You've saved me, old man. But we still have to save Barry."

Jim had come out three hundred feet above the lower entrance. He had to struggle down through tangled scrub. Stones slipped beneath his feet, thorns tore his clothes, he was hungry and dreadfully tired, yet he never stopped until he reached the edge of the clearing. It was dusk now as he crept softly towards the back of the shack.

All was quiet. So Parral, sure that Jim was done for, had not bothered about Barry. Greatly relieved, Jim rose to his feet and walked round to the door. As he reached it a man stepped out. It was Parral.

Parral's surprise was greater than Jim's. He staggered back, his superstitious mind full of sudden terror. His eyes bulged, his yellow face went a sickly green. He had left Jim walled up behind tons of broken rock. This ragged figure with the white face streaked with blood must be his ghost.

Jim's quick mind seized on the reason for Parral's fright, and instead of moving he stood stock still, gazing silently at the brutal half-breed. A gasp of horror whistled between Parral's dry lips, suddenly he turned and ran blindly.

Then Jim made a terrible mistake. Instead of stepping away into the darkness under the wall, he burst into a laugh. Somehow he could not help it.

In a flash Parral stopped, spun round and pulled out a pistol. There was a flash, a crack and Jim ducked as the first bullet whistled past him. From behind him came a hideous snarl. The bullet, missing Jim, had grazed the shoulder of the great puma. All his fury loosed, Pintado leaped forward.

Yelling with terror, Parral fled again. With death at his heels he went straight for the river, reached it one step ahead of the puma and leaped far out into the still water.

Jim racing after, saw the man's dark head rise a dozen yards from the bank, and seized Pintado just in time to stop him from following.

" Come back, you fool," he shouted to Parral, but it was too late. Screaming hideously, Parral flung up his arms and vanished. The pirai, those razor-toothed denizens of the deep creek, had him. As the ripples died Jim turned and went back to the shack where Barry lay, terrified but happily still unharmed.

"He told me you were dead, Jim," Barry said hoarsely.

"But it's he, not I," replied Jim as he dropped, exhausted, on a stool.

T. C. Bridges.

MR. TIGG COMES BACK

" This," said Mr. Duff, " is Mr. Tigg. He used to be a boy here twenty years ago. Since then he's been in Africa and China quite a lot, but he's just looked back to see the old school again, and I'll ask him to say a few words to you."

All looked with interest at the tall bronzed gentleman who smiled genially at them. " Yes, I used to sit on the same forms, learn the same lessons, and play the same games as you do now," he declared, " but the thing I liked to do most of all was to——"

Miaow—wow!

The wail of a cat rang out clearly, and one and all gazed upwards to the skylight which was slightly open. " There's a cat on the roof, sir," exclaimed half a dozen voices at once.

Mr. Duff frowned. " Never mind, boys. Pay attention and——"

Mia-ow—wow—wow—Spph! Ffh! Wow—FFH!

Sounds came as though two more cats had joined in and were having a pitched battle on the school roof, and the boys broke into laughter in spite of the master's glare.

"Hullo, everybody!" boomed a deep voice

"I'm afraid I can't go on until that noise ceases," observed Mr. Tigg. "It's too disturbing." He too was gazing upwards, but there was nothing to be seen.

"Jones," called Mr. Duff sharply to the head boy. "Tell the caretaker to get a ladder and chase those cats away at once."

"Yes, sir," answered Jones, and hurriedly left the room.

"I'll wait until he returns," said Mr. Tigg. He strolled over to the wireless set. "Splendid, having lessons in this way. No such luck in my time. Is anything good on now?" His hand touched a switch as he spoke.

"Hullo everybody," boomed a deep voice. "This is what we call our Special Advice Hour when we give hints of all kinds to people of all kinds. My first word of advice is to teachers. In these fine days don't coop your scholars in. Have as many classes out of doors as possible."

Mr. Duff scratched his head thoughtfully as Mr. Tigg's hand moved to the switch again, and the voice ceased. "Rather good advice, don't you think so, Mr. Duff? Nothing like fresh air for youngsters, eh? Would you like me to give the rest of my talk in the playground?"

"Oh, please do, sir," appealed twenty eager voices in chorus.

"Very well," agreed Mr. Duff.

Jones returned a moment later. "The caretaker has gone to town, sir, and hasn't got back yet."

"Never mind then," said Mr. Duff. "We are going to the playground for the rest of the morning. Get some benches and chairs arranged there as quickly as possible."

A few minutes later the boys had gleefully assembled in the open air, where Mr. Tigg gave a very interesting and amusing account of his adventures abroad, after which the boys gave him a hearty cheer. "I'm sure they listened all the better for having the talk outside," said Mr. Tigg, as he shook hands with his old master. "I'd follow that wireless tip if I were you every fine day."

"I will," responded the master, "in memory of your visit."

On the way home from school several of the boys met the caretaker, Mr. Potts, hurrying along with a very red face. "I hope Mr. Duff hasn't wanted the wireless this morning," he said, " but I've been delayed in getting back. Our car had a breakdown."

" The wireless has been all right to-day," the boys assured him. " At least it was on for a few moments."

" But it can't have," gasped the caretaker. " *It has no batteries! I smashed them this morning accidentally and raced off to town to get new ones!*"

And while the boys stared at him in astonishment, back in his house Mr. Duff with a strange look on his face was turning the pages of the *Wireless News*. " Nothing about Special Advice Hour at eleven," he gurgled. " It should be a lecture by Dr. Drydale on ' People I have met '."

He flung down the paper and thumped his fist on the table in a manner that caused the dinner plates to rattle loudly. " Special Advice! I'd like to advise ventriloquists to keep their tricks for concerts and not play them at schools! My word, I wish Johnnie Tigg was a boy again and I had him here for five minutes! I'd give him wireless—*and cats!*"

O. I. C.

JONES IN LONDON

The chief things about Jones were his size, his games, and his vocabulary.

About the first, if some called him "Fatty" they were mistaken, for his heftiness was hard brawn.

About the second there was no mistake, for most of that Term's successful cricket was due to him.

And as for the third, he had lived all his life in a remote corner of Wales, with a grandfather who compiled dictionaries. Jones had an alternative word for every one he used, like a Crossword Puzzle.

He owned a round and simple countenance, the blandest smile in creation, and a pair of pale blue eyes that missed nothing, which was surprising, for if ever a fellow looked slow, lazy and unperceptive Jones was the one. Coupled with these he was as shy as a rabbit with the Westchester masters, and had an altogether exaggerated reverence for school rules.

Crow, who was his particular friend, gave him advice about his top hat: there wasn't another like it in London, anyway not at any London school.

"Splendid for the old coaching days and all that," said Crow affably, "but not quite so successful here."

"My hat," replied Jones, "is a perfectly good hat——"

"Headgear, head-cover, helmet——", supplied Crow, "see ' Busby '——"

"This hat belonged to my grandfather," asserted Jones. "It would be a pity to waste it—besides, I lay no claim to be a popinjay."

"A *what*?"

"Popinjay, beau, fop, dude or dandyprat," said Jones. "Don't find fault with my hat again, sir, or I shall go off in offence, umbrage, odium or dudgeon."

"Do you wear it in Wales?" asked Crow faintly, "because, if so, I'm not coming to stay with you."

Jones shook his head.

"It is brushed and put away for next term," he said.

Jones was packing his trunk. He and Crow were to catch the night-train from Paddington. He wrapped his pads round his bat with care. The bat

"I say, aren't you finished?"

had played first-class cricket long ago, for like the hat it belonged to Grandfather.

Crow poked his head into the cubicle.

" I say, aren't you finished? There isn't much time, you know."

" Not nearly! I've had awful bad luck—fact was, I packed my beetles by mistake. They'd have died of asphyxia, so I had to unpack again, and now I seem to have twice as many clothes as I had before— is it late?"

" Well, you'd better hurry up—I doubt if you'll do it," said Crow urgently. " Look here, give me your money, and I'll taxi on and get the tickets— train leaves 10.15."

Jones extracted half a crown and handed his wallet to Crow, who dashed away down the dormitory. In a moment he was back.

" Where do I book to?" he asked.

" To Cythbwenthllanrog."

" Gosh!" exploded Crow. " Well—I'll make a noise like a dog fight into the booking office, and hope for the tickets. I say, hurry up!"

Jones was in a frantic muddle; he repacked the trunk till its contents rose high above the rim, added his 1st XI. blazer and subtracted his best trousers. Even now would the thing shut? Like the hat and the bat, the trunk belonged to Grandfather. He cautiously drew the lid down and endeavoured to settle the matter by sitting on it. The immediate result was two sharp reports—the hinges had parted.

Jones ran his fingers through his hair, and then bounded down the dormitory, and knocked timidly at a door.

In the gloaming, Matron's face rose out of a sea of clean linen.

" Why are you so late, Jones?" she exclaimed.

Jones was never at his best in the face of authority; he blushed furiously.

" My trunk," he explained, " has had a slight accident, might I ask the loan of a strap, cord, rope—or—or twine, it's rather urgent."

Later, with baggage of strange appearance, Jones hailed a taxi.

" To Paddington, please—quickly!" he breathed.

The taxi-man wasted one moment in winking one eye, then swinging out of the yard got caught in a traffic block.

Jones's huge form heaved itself round the taxi,

and in feverish anxiety he pushed his head first out of one window and then the other.

" All right, Tiny, only a matter of time," sang out the driver.

The traffic moved on, the taxi darted down a side turning, made a short cut, and dived into Paddington. A slow-looking porter opened the door; Jones paid the fare of two shillings, and snatched up his pads and beetles.

" Ten fifteen to Cythbwenthllanrog!" he shouted.

" She's gorn," said the porter dismally.

Jones sat down under the clock and meditated. Then he got up slowly and made his way to the booking office.

" Can you tell me," he said, " whether a fellow in a hat like mine took two tickets to Cythbwenth-llanrog just now?"

The booking-office clerk laid his face on the counter and looked up at the hat through the wires of his cage.

" It was something like yours," he said. " Here's the ticket, he sent it back by a porter."

" The next train leaves——?"

" 9.15 to-morrow morning," said the clerk.

JONES IN LONDON

It was difficult. Jones had no friends in London and Term was over. He remembered reading in the school rules that no boy was permitted to remain on the premises for a night after the last day of Term. Jones had a reverence for rules that amounted to fear. It had needed special permission for him and Crow to remain for the last train, and Matron had been very unamiable about the trunk. Jones was timid as a fly at such moments, official disapproval was worse than Whipsnade let loose.

The voice of the porter roused him.

" These 'ere for the cloakroom?" he enquired.

" Please," said Jones.

He disposed of his luggage, beetles and last sixpence, and walked out of the station.

Crow had no friends in London either and so had gone on. Not that it would have mattered very much to Crow, he would have gone boldly back to school and explained matters.

The thought made Jones turn hot and then cold, but of course it must be done. London was not like Wales, where you could stay out all night on the lap of some homely old mountain. But it would take time to walk back, and he would be fearfully late.

Nevertheless, Jones was an optimist, and, as a man of the wild, always liked a bit of adventure. It was rather novel to be out and yet not out of bounds—the night would pass and to-morrow it would be over—next term it would be miles away in the past. He began to think of next term—and keeping goal for the first eleven. Boxing too. The only chap he was allowed to box was old Bindle, the instructor. He was always just about to do his worst to Bindle when the old champion would say:

"That's enough, Mr. Jones, sir—I think you've had enough, Mr. Jones."

A smile of pleasant recollection spread over his face, and his spirits went up. What would Crow do if he were in Jones's shoes to-night? Get some magnanimous motorist to give him a quick lift back to school—splendid idea!

A car was drawn up at the kerb. Jones muttered a word of wonder and eyed it from behind. Undoubtedly a Moore-Morrison, one of the new models —new since the Show.

Jones in the moonlight blushed down to his collar as he put his head into the window.

"I say, Sir, excuse me—I wonder if you're going

in the direction of Westchester — and if so —— "

" No," replied a voice.

Jones blinked in confusion.

" Er—sorry—— ", he murmured, and shot off down the nearest turning which led him into a deserted arcade. He realized it would take him out to the short cut the taxi had taken. On each side the black corrugated shutters of shops rose, and the moonlight was dimmed by the glass overhead. At one point an iron grid shielded a low door. Jones noted that it was slightly ajar, then a pencil line of light gleamed along the door and went out. Jones put one of his pale blue eyes to the crack. The next moment he was shoved violently forward. The door fell back on a figure that had evidently been ready to open it, and closed quietly behind him with the turn of a key. Another man was behind him.

Jones blinked. The whole thing had been the work of a moment. He stepped back and took in the situation. A dark lantern on the floor made a splash of light, but the gleam was caught and reflected by a number of bright stones in trays lying about in disorder—a jeweller's!

Two men were regarding him in the queer half-light: he had never seen that look before, the look of a man who has everything to lose if he is caught, or if he hesitates. Not a word was spoken as they measured him with those odd, quick glances.

Jones sat down in a limp heap on a chair, and the sharpness of the glances relaxed.

The man beside him laughed quietly.

" Large, but not formidable," he remarked. " I guessed it was not official—but still——"

They were extraordinarily quick with their hands. Jones had seen conjurers produce things from nowhere—but ropes and a gag—no, nothing as bulky as these. Jones gently removed his hat, and laid it on the counter. Then he stood up lazily, hands in pockets. It was a pretty nobby knot the fellow was tying—once inside that—a light was switched on, but not a ray would penetrate into the arcade.

" Hands up—we're two to one!"

With the next movement the man on the left reeled back, and crashed to the floor with a stunning blow under the chin, followed a lightning upper-cut on man number two, with less success.

Jones was on his toes; he had suddenly grown trim and light, he had yet to discover if either could

He floored the first man again

box, but as for him, he felt the excitement of the thing tingling pleasantly. They would try to get out—pity if they escaped, the key was in the lock—good thing no guns had appeared—biff! The wary figure was on guard again in an instant—no use hitting wildly, every well-placed blow was worth any number of false ones. He floored the first man again—just as well when there are two. No, no, not into the corners, he regained the centre with some skill and sent his man head backwards through a glass case, and had the other tottering before the first regained his feet.

(" Steady, Mr. Jones, sir, I think you've had enough.")

Funny he'd been thinking of old man Bindle—enough for one round possibly, but these fellows didn't play any known game—they were fairly mad now, but the big figure still danced on its toes. Jones's pale eyes were measuring, calculating, aiming, his cat-like movements preventing foul play. He had taken them by surprise, he knew that had counted to him from the first. He regained the door, and a crash of glass followed as a figure collapsed through a second show case, and did not seem inclined to get out of it.

("Mr. Jones, sir, you've had enough——"

"My dear Bindle, only just warming up, I assure you——"

"Beautiful footwork, Mr. Jones—nice, very nice. Break away! No holding!"

"Sorry, Bindle, I've got to hold, I've got to tie him up—awfully nobby knot—that's it—now the one over there. Gosh! what a mess!")

Jones sat down. His head was like a merry-go-round, and he was panting like a dog. Whew! it was hot! He drew out his handkerchief and slowly mopped himself up, then his head began to buzz round again, and he sat with a pair of unsightly knuckles on his knees—how long? Anyway, the chaps on the floor perked up first and roused him. They were not being complimentary!

Jones stood up. He was perfectly all right now—and he must do something. Couldn't go out and fetch a policeman, altogether too public—he was in Westchester clothes. He walked out of the department and found an office, picked up a telephone receiver and asked for Scotland Yard. That was a great idea! No one would know a mere voice, his spirits went up and he gurgled back a satisfied chuckle.

" At the premises of Messrs. Bridge of Mitre Street, W., you will find two gentlemen who are not quite in the pink. . . . I said the pink—they are on the floor, jewellery is spread in a lavish manner about them—I said jewellery, stones or baubles. I fear they are felonious persons, thieves or low fellows. Round the corner in Reem's Street you may or may not find a car, a new Moore-Morrison, No. C.44458, left back mudguard slightly damaged. I am in a hurry—to catch a train—you will find the light switched off, and the door on the latch, enter through the arcade. Pardon? My name? My name, sir, is Jones, and I am not in the telephone book—goodnight, officer."

The sun rose over Westchester playing fields, the early morning resort of London sparrows by the hundred. On the Pavilion roof half a dozen pigeons were turning circles and practising arpeggios. They roused Jones. He had funked going back to school at an unusual and unseemly hour of the night, in a state of untidiness and disorder, and had made for the playing fields and pavvy. He had slept like a log on a bench, and woke wondering what ailed his left ear and his right hand knuckles.

The rooms were locked up. He walked stiffly round on the outside, and noted a window unlatched. In there was cold water and a towel! Placing his hands on the high sill he sprang up, and with difficulty squeezed himself in. Water! He removed his collar, and spent ten excellent minutes; discovered a comb, noted his ear in a glass, replaced collar and tie, and became aware that he was hungry. Nothing in his pockets but a railway ticket, obviously inedible; nothing in prospect but a journey on a train that reeked of breakfast—and the journey would take all day. He looked round—a limp and aged blazer hung on a peg, he turned it round, Crow's old one.

After searching it Jones sat down and fanned himself with his hat. Two terms ago Crow had lost a 10s. note—it was in the pocket.

The guard's whistle sounded loud and long. Hat, bat and beetles were safely on the rack. Jones blinking at a headline in the morning paper.

" Two of the most skilful thieves in London found bound in famous jeweller's. Hospital treatment. Mysterious telephone message. Police hunt for Jones."

4

" They'll never find Cythbwenthllanrog," he murmured.

The waiter darted down the corridor and poked a cheery face into the carriage.

" Which breakfast will you take, sir? Fried eggs—bacon—and—mushrooms — coffee — toast — marmalade."

" Or?" queried Jones, mastering a wolfish gleam.

" Haddock—poached eggs—sausages—omelette—hot rolls—strawberry jam."

" Both," said Jones, " at your earliest convenience."

N. Humphry Davy.

THE CALL OF DUTY

Billy Farquhar admitted to himself that he was afraid of the water. True, he had sometimes been to the swimming baths, but he had done nothing but splash about with one hand on the chains; he had felt that if he let go he would slip on the shiny white tiles and his head would go under.

So, when the time came for him to go to boarding-school, it was perhaps unfortunate that his father should send him to Riverside College, which was within a stone's throw of the River *Wander*, and where aquatic sports were a big feature.

At Riverside, every boy has to " pass out " in swimming before he is allowed to bathe or go on the river in even the roomiest and most unsinkable of craft. But a mere " pass " is insufficient to label you a " wetter "; every boy who is worth his salt goes on to qualify for his life-saving badge. That much is almost compulsory, but in addition there is the traditional custom which insists that, at least once during the summer half, all but the " kids " must dive or jump from Swallow Bridge—so called from the resemblance its two low arches are supposed to bear to a swallow in flight.

Billy did manage at last to get his " pass-out " and badge, but no one but himself knew what the effort cost him. The bridge dive he simply refused to contemplate—it was utterly beyond him. He told himself that " bridging ", as it was called, was just a silly custom which had no value. Besides, it was risky. Since he had been at Riverside there had been two accidents which might have proved serious. Jumping in too near the side, Fatty Baynes had broken a finger on the stonework, and Jimmy Carter had funked just as he was " taking-off " for a dive, with the result that he had fallen flat and knocked all the breath out of his body. He had only just managed to reach the bank. Billy thought that it ought to be forbidden, and had said so to some of his form mates; but they had laughed at him. According to Tony Yorke, it was " an immemorial custom " (Tony was fond of long words) at Riverside, and there would certainly be a mutiny in the school if an attempt was made to stop it. There was, said Tony, a similar custom at Eton. Billy had urged that it was dangerous, and had instanced the case of Jimmy Carter.

If Jimmy had been alone, and if he had been quite stunned instead of only half stunned, he might have been drowned.

But Tony had merely laughed and said, " Oh, *if—if——*" whilst Bob Harker had remarked cruelly, " Serve the blighter right! Only funks dive flat."

So Billy, fearful lest that dreaded name should be applied to him, had quickly changed the subject.

Whenever he crossed Swallow Bridge to reach Middle Mallows, he halted and looked doubtfully at the river flowing calmly below. It was not really a great height—little more than from the top diving-board in the swimming-baths at home, but to the eyes of one who rarely dived, but just slid shamefully into the water from the bank, it seemed a fearful drop. He always walked on with the feeling that, however long he stayed at Riverside, Swallow Bridge would always be too much for him.

In one of his letters home, he told his father about the bridge and how he felt unable to do what most of his schoolmates did.

In his reply his father said, " Don't worry about that bridge business. Physical courage is good but moral courage is better, and I would be sorry to see

4*

you do things merely because they were usual. Respect the rules but otherwise take a line of your own. It is no disgrace to fear danger; true courage doesn't consist of showing off but of overcoming fear at the call of duty. And don't start thinking you are a funk; I am sure that, if the need arose, you would show as much pluck as any of those reckless young fellows you mention!"

This letter heartened Billy considerably and he decided to put the matter from his mind; after all, there was no compulsion. If Bob Harker and his crowd liked to think him a funk—well, let them. They wouldn't *call* him one with impunity.

And then came the fateful autumn evening which he was never to forget. He was crossing the bridge and had paused for his usual scared glance down, when he noticed a small urchin sitting on the bank and splashing his feet in the water. There was a shelving bank just at that spot, but a yard away, as Billy well knew, it was nearly six feet deep. Quite possibly the urchin could swim, but if he couldn't and he slipped in—— Billy felt a chill down the back—not, it must be admitted, at what might happen to the urchin, but at what would certainly happen to

And then it happened

himself. He would be despised because he had had a chance to save a life and had funked.

Presently he heard footsteps and, turning, saw Bob Harker approaching. Bob stopped and peered over the coping to see what was the attraction, but he chose a spot some distance away. Billy flushed, but he was not surprised; Bob was one of the " bloods "— a chap who dared anything. It would hardly do for him to pal up with a fellow who shirked "bridging".

" Suppose the kid *did* fall in—what could I do?" thought Billy, and he answered himself bitterly, " Run for help, that's all. And before I got back Bob would have gone in and fished him out."

Suddenly it struck him that he had better get on before he was put to the test. Kids did fall in sometimes. He straightened himself and turned to move on——

And then it happened. A third-former on a push-bike suddenly shot on to the bridge, caught his front wheel on Bob's outstretched legs, went off at a tangent, collided with the opposite side and was shot neatly out of his saddle over the coping. It takes a long sentence to describe it but it happened in a second.

THE CALL OF DUTY

Almost before the boy had struck the water there was a shrill cry of " Help!", followed by running footsteps and a second splash.

Five minutes later a sixth-former, taking a practice run along the towing-path, came on a soaked and panting fourth-former vainly endeavouring to administer first-aid to an equally soaked and apparently drowned schoolmate.

" Here, let me!" cried the senior, and he proceeded to go through the appointed movements.

He worked feverishly for some minutes without result, then gave an exclamation of triumph.

" There, see that? His eyelids fluttered."

Suddenly his patient began to cough, and presently essayed to sit up.

" Steady!" said the senior. " Take your time." Then he looked round at the other boy, who was shivering violently. " You'd better cut off now and get changed. Did you get him out?"

" Yes."

" What's your name?"

" Farquhar," said Billy.

A. W. Seymour.

" JAMMY "

I

Those who hear our little stocky stand-off half, Sinclair, addressed by or referred to as " Jammy ", wonder how on earth he came by a nickname that seems so utterly inappropriate for the man. Even at St. Serf's most of us have forgotten the story of its origin. One or two, however, are not likely to do so. David Sinclair himself is undoubtedly amongst these, and so are Fyfe and Rankin and Shaftesbury. These four have good reason to remember it. There were others in the secret, but they have left.

There is, I may say, a superficial explanation current. At the sports last year, when Sinclair had just won the quarter amongst yells of " Come on, Jam!" and " Well run, Jammy!" I heard the mother of a small squirt in the Third ask her dear little son why that nice-looking boy had such a funny nickname, and the kid replied, " I dunno. I suppose it was because he likes the stuff—and by the bye, mother, I hope you'll send more of that greengage kind next term. It's jolly good but it doesn't last."

The kid was right enough as far as he went, but

that went by no means to the root of the matter. Of course Sinclair liked jam, what human creature doesn't? His fondness for jam wouldn't have been enough to make it stick to him for ever as it seems likely to do. No, that's by no means the whole story.

Sinclair was rather a funny chap when he first came to St. Serf's. He had come straight from some prep. school in Scotland, and had a way of speaking that got him chaffed a lot. As he had also a very quick temper, he had more than a spot of bother for his first month or two. He was as brave as a tiger, and would lash out at fellows who could have licked him with one hand if they had taken him seriously. He took *them* seriously, that was his way; he hadn't got used to being chaffed, and I suppose the fellows didn't understand him or they'd have gone easy.

Well, in those days the grub at St. Serf's wasn't as good as it is now, and we didn't have jam every day. Fellows who brought jam in their tuck boxes were allowed to have it at tea, and of course every chap who had a stock would share it with his chums till it was gone.

Sinclair hadn't any chums at first, his beastly

independence and his fiery temper prevented it, but he had a wonderful supply of home-made cranberry jam. It was priceless stuff—I never knew anything it was so fine to eat too much of. (We discovered this in the end, when Sinclair's education had proceeded a bit, and this stormy period of his career was over.)

Day after day he sat at tea with his pot of cranberry jam beside his plate, with his name on it, and tucked into it while the rest of us shared jams and jellies of more ordinary kinds. Even the master in charge of our table seemed to notice that Sinclair's pot was never shoved along to anybody else. I remember seeing him—a chap named Crawshaw—looking at the Scots boy as if he were an egg of doubtful freshness.

One day this habit of Sinclair's got too much for some of us, and somebody just grabbed his cranberry jam, and saying loudly, " Thank you, Sinclair, I don't mind if I do," took a huge helping and passed the pot along.

Sinclair flared up at once and began to make a row, but Crawshaw told him to be quiet. I don't know if he knew just what had happened, but anyhow what he said was, " Not so much noise, Sinclair. Surely you can pass round your jam without setting the table in a riot?"

And Sinclair had to subside, though his cheeks were flaring, and I knew we hadn't heard the last of it. The pot came back to him with just a few spoonfuls of jam in it, and everybody chuckled to think how Sinclair had been scored over.

I remembered afterwards that as he stalked off alone to prep—I was just behind him—I overheard him humming to himself a Scots tune. It was " Loch Lomond". Had I known the man then as well as I've come to know him since, I should have been aware that the jam incident wasn't closed, and been on my guard. When Sinclair hums that, look out for squalls. The further off the tune he is, the more deeply he's thinking, and the worse the trouble for somebody.

Well, when we turned in that night, there was no end of a row in the dormitory. Something was wrong with my pyjamas: they were all sticky between the shoulders. About half a dozen chaps found the same—and we discovered that jam, just a little, but enough to be beastly uncomfortable—had been well rubbed into them. There was a touch of it else-where, we found—inside a sleeve or a leg. Almost as soon as we began to suspect Sinclair, he jumped up on his bed and said, " I thought you might as well have the rest of the pot. Sorry there wasn't more."

That started a rough house all night, and though Sinclair was a tough chap even then he would have had a pretty bad time had not one of the prefects come in and chased us all into bed. He wasn't a fellow to be trifled with, so nothing more happened that night.

" Just you wait, Sinclair," somebody said by way of good-night. " We'll teach you to spread jam on people's clothes."

" I don't need teaching, do I?" Sinclair retorted. " Lick it off, since you like it so much."

" Just you wait," came back the reply, and Sinclair had the last word with, " Well, I'm waiting, aren't I?"

It seemed to some of us that we were all square, and that Sinclair had had a sporting revenge and should be left alone, but some of the bigger chaps, including Fyfe and Rankin, said he wasn't going to get away with a trick like that, and put their heads together over a plan for revenge.

The rest of us didn't know what it was going to be till we saw it carried out. It was very well planned, and Sinclair really had no chance to resist. Just after he'd got into bed one night half a dozen of them jumped on him simultaneously and held him tight. He put up a rare struggle, but it wasn't any good, and though a yell or two would have brought in a prefect or the housemaster, they knew even then that Sinclair would keep as quiet as possible just for that very reason.

Some of us were rather sorry for him, but it wasn't our job to interfere—and, anyhow, we knew nothing very dreadful was going to happen to him. Well, they made him sit up and pulled off his pyjama jacket, and while two held his legs, two his arms, and one his head the sixth produced a two-pound pot of strawberry jam, and smeared the stuff all over the poor beggar's head and face and back and shoulders. You never saw a funnier sight than poor old Sinclair. He took it very calmly. When the job was done, and they all let go and stood back, we expected him to go berserk and try to fight the whole lot, but he just sat still for a minute, wiping jam out of his eyes, and getting more in off his knuckles as he did so.

" That's all for yourself, my Hieland laddie," said Shaftesbury. " It mayn't be cranberry, but strawberry's not too bad, is it?"

Sinclair didn't say anything, but he gave Shaftesbury a glare that looked all the fiercer because of the mask of jam around his eyes. Then he got up slowly and marched out of the dormitory. Was he going to squeal to somebody? Not he—we guessed that whatever he was he wasn't yellow. No, he just went along to the bathroom to dejam himself. Some of the chaps were asleep before he came back. It was no wonder he took a long time, for Shaftesbury had worked the jam well in, hair, ears, everywhere, including the small of his back. My bed was next to his, and though I was a bit sleepy, I heard him come back—and again he was jerkily humming something intended to be " Loch Lomond "—terribly off the notes.

II

After that Sinclair began to settle down. We discovered that he could play rugger, and was really a decent chap all round, and I suppose he began to understand us a bit. Anyhow he was soon one of the gang, and shared his cranberry jam with a crowd of pals which grew steadily in size.

The jam-painting episode was pretty well forgotten, but other people besides myself noticed what I've mentioned about the song " Loch Lomond ", that when Sinclair hummed snatches of it his Scots blood was up and somebody had better look out. I've heard him often at it at half-time, when a game was going against St. Serf's, and it always meant that Sinclair played like two men, and desperate ones at that, in the second half. And I remembered how I had heard some distorted bars of the tune when he came back clean to bed that night.

Next year he, and those other fellows I've mentioned, moved into studies, and were all pretty good friends. They were allowed to have tea there if they liked, and so they'd ask one another in when one study was well-off for grub, and so forth. Sinclair and I and a chap Mason shared a study, and got on together first-rate. Consignments of cranberry jam still came for Sinclair, and Mason and I developed such a taste for it that we are still absolute cranberry-hounds. No cranberry in any form is safe when we're about. However, that has nothing much to do with the story.

One day Mason and I were having tea with some other crowd, and Sinclair mentioned that he had asked some beggars to have tea with him in our absence. We drifted back just as they were finishing. Fyfe and Rankin were amongst them. They'd had a glorious gorge—anybody could see that by the way they were sprawling about, one and all with that distended look which does a host's heart good to see.

" Fed well? " Fyfe said to us. " There's nowhere to sit but the floor. We can't move. It's Sandy's fault "—most of us called him Sandy then, because he was a Scot. Only a few very intimate friends called him " Jammy "—the rest didn't think he'd care to be reminded of that sticky night.

" You gluttonous brutes," Mason answered. " I suppose you've finished all our cranberry jam. Mac, you'll have to send the fiery cross home for another cargo of it."

" As a matter of fact," Sinclair answered, with a one-sided grin characteristic of him when he was being funny, " I didn't give 'em cranberry to-night—strawberry for a change. Was it all right, you chaps?

" Sandy, you hound!"

You liked it? Did you notice its real Scotch flavour?"

" Jam was all right," grunted someone; " O.K.", another; and " Great Stuff ", a third.

" Strawberry," went on Sinclair, in a sort of dreamy way. " Strawberry jam. Wonderful how it will keep with a little preservative added. . . . But oh, it's sticky! Very hard to scrape out of a man's hair, for instance, particularly if he's an honest Scot and wants to return all of it to its owners!"

Shaftesbury had been lolling with his knees against the underside of the table and his chair tilted back. Suddenly he swung forward and the chair's front legs came down with a thump.

" Sandy, you hound! We've eaten the jam we pasted over you that night in your first term!"

You should have seen how the rest of them woke up, and the change of their expressions when they remembered and realized. I never saw fellows look so queer. One, at least, turned green. I think they felt almost like cannibals.

" Oh, my aunt!" groaned Rankin, " and I never ate strawberry jam I liked so much."

" A very pretty compliment," Sinclair grinned. " You say we Scots are economical—don't say I didn't scrape to provide you with a good spread."

" Chuck it, for the love of Mike!" said Fyfe—it was he who was greenest—" unless you want me to be ill in here."

For a minute I wondered how they'd all take it—I wasn't sure of a couple of them, but it was Fyfe—all honour to him—who decided for the lot.

" I think you must excuse me—and rather quickly, Sinclair," he said, " but ere staggering out let me say that I think you've won. You've waited, but you've won. Gentleman, however queer you're feeling— hasn't Sandy won?"

By word or sign—several seemed not to trust themselves to speak, they agreed: at the same time there was a unanimous yearning to depart. The joke on them was too fresh—it hadn't yet been properly digested!—and there was a general movement to the door.

Sandy winked at me and watched them for a moment, and then he spoke again.

" What's your hurry?" he said, " I never said that was the same strawberry jam, did I? Pretty poor judges of jam you must be. Hang it, you plastered me with foul bought stuff—turnip pulp and birdseed. If you didn't recognize real home-made to-night you don't deserve what's good for you! The mater ran out of cranberry and sent me her own strawberry instead. But I had you properly, hadn't I?"

Then, suddenly cured, they fell upon him with playful whoops and sat on him in boisterous brotherli-ness. And that is really how Sinclair got the name " Jammy."

W. K. Holmes.

ZULU JU-JU

Kisimoyu, on the east coast of Africa, is roughly forty miles south of the equator. Forty miles north of Kisimoyu, one December night, three men reclined on the sandy sea shore, in various attitudes of prostration, round the glowing embers of a log fire. On the one side rose the sheer black wall of the jungle, from which came the inevitable African medley; a conglomeration of animal noises, far and near, a mighty, pulsating murmur, pierced ever and anon by the individual call of a nocturnal hunter. On the other side the sea thundered and sighed, crashing its huge breakers on to the shore as if in angry defiance of the jungle roar.

John Ferrier, the larger of the two Englishmen at the fire, exerted himself sufficiently to attend to the funeral of a foolishly persistent mosquito which had found its way through the net.

" Phew!" he gasped, flopping back again, " never known it so hot. Can't sleep. 'Quator, and midsummer—bad management, eh, Jerry?"

Jerry Weston grinned, the flickering light from the

fire, several yards away, showing a myriad creases in his lean, parchment-like cheerful face. He was smaller and leaner than his partner, and could better afford to smile at the roasting tropical heat.

"Don't blame anyone but John, my lad," he chuckled. "The power of your will brought us here against the counsel of the wise, namely, the Ethiopian Lumbangu and my humble self, and now your unwieldy bulk will jolly well have to put up with the consequences."

"Brr!" grunted Ferrier, "'unwieldy bulk'! I like that! Why, you're nothing but a strip of biltong! Jealousy, that's what it is. If those Kasinki pigmies in the Congo had staked you out in the sun as they intended that time last year, my son, you wouldn't have dried up any more. You're just for all the world like a fillet of old rhino hide!"

Which latter remark was certainly more correct than that made by Jerry. John Ferrier was certainly "bulky"—he weighed fourteen stones—but he was anything except unwieldy. He was all huge bone and muscle, as strong as a gorilla, and could move as swiftly as a panther when the occasion demanded.

Jerry, on the other hand, was small, lean and wiry,

and just as tough as the rhinoceros hide to which the indignant John Ferrier had likened him.

The third member of the party, and obviously the least affected by the heat, rose to his feet, his black face creased into a broad grin.

"Bwanas have palaver fight. Lumbangu not wanted. Go now, have ju-ju palaver. Come back soon."

The giant Zulu lifted his hand, turned lithely, and melted into the night.

"Quaint beggar!" exclaimed Jerry, gazing into the darkness where Lumbangu had vanished. "I'd have thought he would be too intelligent to believe in that ju-ju stuff. He's far and away more brainy than the average Kaffir."

Ferrier did not answer for some minutes. Older than his companion, he had learned to know the mind of the African native intimately, and was less apt to scoff at some of their queer habits and rituals than those white men who judged from a rather narrow western standpoint, without attempting to understand.

"Lumbangu's one of the best," said Ferrier at length. "He's a white man in everything except his skin, and he's the only African native I've ever been able to treat as an equal. Usually if you give 'em half an inch they start regarding you as a darn fool, and you have to kick 'em back to reason again, but not Lumbangu. He's too brainy to lose his head, and he's got too much sense to bother about ju-ju if there were nothing in it. Africa's full of things I don't understand, and ju-ju's one of them."

Jerry grunted non-committally, and turned the conversation.

" I suppose we start prospecting to-morrow?" he said, and when Ferrier nodded, added, " The rains are just about due, so after being scorched up, we shall all be washed into the sea, and everything in the garden will be lovely. I wish you'd got your information about this gold reef six months later, my lad!"

They talked on for an hour about one thing and another, but mainly the gold for which they were prospecting, until Lumbangu suddenly appeared out of the black wall of the night as silently as he had vanished.

He piled logs on the fire, and set about making supper. Presently curiosity got the better of Jerry,

and as he sipped the strong tea which Lumbangu
handed to him, he asked a question which the
average native would not have answered, since they
never discuss their "ju-ju".

"Well, you old heathen, was the jolly old ju-ju
fizzin' right to-night? Has it told you where our
gold reef is?"

To John Ferrier's surprise, Lumbangu answered
the question promptly.

"Bwana laugh. Lumbangu no laugh. Bwana
no laugh any more when big tusker take um by
hand and say 'Here is much wealth for Bwanas'.
Ju-ju say Bwanas not to shoot big tusker."

After which cryptic utterance Lumbangu tabooed
the subject, and neither Jerry nor Ferrier could get
another word out of him. He had been very serious
about it, and evidently meant to convey that an
elephant would take them "by the hand" and lead
them to the gold, and that no elephant must be
shot, or their means of finding the gold would be
destroyed.

For three days the trio carried on the thirsty
task of prospecting for gold along the sea shore.
They were able to work only in the morning and late

afternoon, for in the middle of the day the heat was so intense that they had to spend some five hours under the shade afforded by the thick growth at the edge of the jungle.

It was in the afternoon of the fourth day. Lumbangu was in the jungle looking for small game for the stew pot, and the two Englishmen were about to recommence prospecting. They had been discussing the advisability of giving up the search, for they had thoroughly worked the locality where Ferrier had reason to believe the gold reef lay. They had completely forgotten about Lumbangu's elephant ju-ju.

They were making their way along the beach to the place where they had ceased operations that morning, when there was a sudden ear-splitting yell from the edge of the bush, and a great black figure leaped into view and sprinted with incredible speed toward the sea. Close behind him—for it was Lumbangu—charged the huge bulk of an enormous bull elephant, and despite the Zulu's amazing speed, the tusker was gaining rapidly.

Jerry's rifle was up in a flash, but as he was about to press the trigger, Ferrier spoke.

" Don't shoot, Jerry—yet. Keep the bead on

Close behind him charged an enormous bull elephant

him, but there'll be no need to kill him. Look!"

As he finished Lumbangu reached the water, the bull almost on his heels. Leaping through the surf, the Zulu dived and swam out. His speed was nothing short of phenomenal, but the weight of the elephant carried it into deep water just as quickly, and the great trunk was raised to crush its victim with a smashing blow, when—the Zulu dived and vanished.

Trumpeting with rage, the elephant turned and made for the shore. Jerry lowered the rifle and made for cover, accompanied by Ferrier.

" Old Ebony's all right. He's like a stickleback in the water. Mr. Tusks'll turn his attention to us if we don't imitate bamboos fairly quickly. Thank goodness we're down-wind."

It was Jerry who spoke. They reached cover, and looked back. Through the leaves they saw the bull reach the beach, turn and scan the sea, and lift his trunk up to trumpet his annoyance once more. Then he turned majestically and stalked off back into the jungle. Ferrier had turned his eyes to the place where Lumbangu had dived, and Jerry heard him catch his breath. The next instant there was a crashing explosion in his ear as Ferrier's gun went off, and a tiny triangle which had appeared in the sea leaped forward convulsively and disappeared in a flurry of threshed-up water. Three yards away Lumbangu's arm appeared above the water, and there was the flash of steel in the sunlight.

Even if Ferrier's bullet had not found its mark, it seemed that the shark would not have had matters entirely its own way!

A moment later the Zulu was ploughing his way toward the beach, using a peculiar overhand stroke which gave him almost the appearance of skimming along the surface of the water. In two minutes he was striding through the surf, but even in that short time two more dorsal fins appeared, evidently investigating the remains of the first shark.

Lumbangu came towards the Englishmen, his even teeth exposed in a broad smile. As he drew nearer they saw a large dark-coloured flat object in his left hand. As they advanced to meet him, he waved the thing aloft.

Jerry could afford to grin now, though both he and Ferrier were keeping a weather eye on the jungle, for there was a chance of the bull coming to investigate the cause of the rifle shot.

" Your ju-ju seems to have played you a dirty trick, King Coal," chuckled Jerry. " So far from leading you to our gold reef, he nearly led you to the sharks, apart from the doubtfulness of the treatment you would have received if he'd got his trunk to you before you did your famous submarine act!"

Lumbangu shook his woolly head emphatically.

" Ju-ju very much right, Bwana. Lumbangu look for buck, big tusker him come, all cross, chase Lumbangu into sea, Lumbangu dive down, down, down, to get 'way from tusks, find number one size pearl oyster. Many more there, same as oyster beds where Lumbangu used to dive years ago."

" Pearl oyster!" exclaimed Ferrier. " I know you used to dive for 'em on the preserves at one time, you black rascal; but how d'you know there are pearls in these?"

" Ju-ju!" said Lumbangu, simply. " See, Bwana!"

Lumbangu had taken his knife from his loin cloth, and with a deft twist of the blade opened the shell. Another quick twist, and in his hand rolled a beautiful pearl, rose-pink, and the size of a hazel nut.

" Great pip!" ejaculated Ferrier, " that must be worth a small fortune alone. A few more of those

"That must be worth a small fortune alone!"

and there'll be no need to hunt for any gold reefs!"

Jerry solemnly held his hand out, and Lumbangu grasped it in his huge black fist.

" I don't know how you do it, Ebony, but you've got Old Moore whacked to a frazzle." He turned to Ferrier. " But how're we to get those oysters up? Look at the sharks!"

" There's plenty of tackle to overcome that difficulty," said Ferrier. " If Lumbangu's report is accurate, we've struck a very valuable unworked oyster bed.

He paused for a moment, then smiled at Jerry.

" Now what about ' that ju-ju stuff '?" he said. " If Lumbangu hadn't told us about it the other night, I'd have let you pip the old bull before they reached the water, and the oyster bed would have remained undiscovered!"

Keith Orme.

JIM'S POLAR PARTY

" I say, Bob," Jim said one Saturday morning, with a wide grin at his chum: " hunt up our crowd and say that I've changed my mind about the dorm feast to-night and that I'm running a polar party in Foster's cave instead. This late snowfall is just the thing for an Arctic expedition."

" Br-rh!" shivered Bob. " You expedish on your own; it's bed for me on a March night."

" Oh no, it isn't, my boy," argued the other, still grinning mischievously. " At least, not until we've had some fine jinks. So you just do as I tell you about the rest of the dorm."

" I believe your uncle's postal order has gone to your head," grumbled Bob. " Why on earth shift to-night's scene of action from comfort to discomfort and risk being missed, into the bargain? Bet you anything the other chaps won't turn out."

" Oh yes, they will!" Jim's tone was confident. " You just say ' Up, St. John's!' because my polar party is for the express purpose of getting rid of Bully Bond."

" Getting *rid* of him! How?" Bob's eyes fairly

bulged, as if he thought the term might mean actually *killing* the village bugbear, a hobbledehoy who had forced his unwelcome services upon the local football and cricket teams and did his best to spoil sport whenever the St. John's teams played them.

" I can't stay to tell you now, because I've things to arrange," Jim replied hastily; " but you can take it from me that I've just been overhearing enough to cook Bully's goose if we can catch him out in a certain act. See you later," and Jim was off village-wards again, leaving a mystified Bob to the job of mystifying others.

The Saturday afternoon's diligence of some of the boys in clearing snow from the school's precincts might have been understood by the masters if they could have seen Jim's party noiselessly sliding down the rails of the outside emergency staircase just before twelve that night. Jim had no mind that footprints in the vicinity should tell tales next morning of the quarter mile sprint to the seashore.

His chums found that they had no reason to complain of the feast Jim had supplied through an Uncle's benevolence, even though they had to turn out into the cold for it. But it was warm enough

I flopped in the snow and listened

round the bucket coke fire he had in an inner cavern of the big cave in the cliffs, and as they all contentedly munched and toasted themselves, he thrilled them with his story.

" Knowing about the smuggling which has been going on lately along this coast," he said; " you can guess how I pricked up my ears when I was snooking through the woods close to the lane this morning and heard Bully's voice telling somebody something about Foster's cave. I simply flopped in the snow among the bushes and listened. He was talking to a man inside a car and I managed to wriggle near enough to hear Bully tell him not to make any mistakes, there would be no moon to-night, so everything ought to be O.K. That the stuff would be landed at high tide, about 1 a.m., that he, Bully, would get it into the cave and have it packed for the different destinations in an hour. So the chap in the car was to come along about two, hide his bus in the cove and they'd load it together.

" Ho! ho! Smuggler Bond!" I said to myself. " Not if St. John's know it, and right on the spot I planned this polar party on purpose to catch him. You see, we shall be wiping out a lot of grievances, and he'll never know who gave him away," and Jim went on to explain a plan of action that drew delighted chuckles from his party.

Curiosity regarding a packet which he had served out to each boy was soon satisfied, and nobody would have recognized pupils of St. John's in the masked and muffled figures wearing top coats inside out, that presently haunted the shadows of the outer cave, waiting for the warning hiss from Jim, which would mean " pounce ".

It came at last, a welcome sound which broke a tension of nearly half an hour, the only sounds during that time being an occasional smothered cough from someone just below who dangled a big lantern in the lee of the cliff, and the thump of the waves, until the beaching scrape of what was evidently an electrically run boat, so silent had been its approach, told that the signal had guided the modern smugglers aright. Then after a few minutes, there had been another scrape as the boat was pushed out to sea again and every boy had stood ready to spring as soon as the unsuspecting Bully Bond should step inside the cave with his first load of smuggled goods.

Jim's dark niche was close to the entrance and he

followed his warning with a wild bound and a snatch at Bully's swinging lantern, the others jumping almost in the same instant to bear the rascal to the sandy floor and get busy with the gag and ropes they had ready.

It was all done with a speed and quietness that must have dumbfounded the victim. Not a word escaped the boys, only their hard breathing testifying to their excitement and efforts. Having secured their quarry, off shot Bob according to orders already received, and five minutes later saw him inside a telephone booth calling coastguard and police stations.

Before very long beach and cave were a scene of animation, for, acting on the information given by the boys, the authorities had lain in wait and captured the motorist accessory.

" Caught redhanded, by gad!" cried one of the coastguards presently, taking time for an interested stare about for the masked figures who had given the alarm and been so active in assisting to carry the contraband goods to the commandeered car for safe custody. " We've been trying for weeks to find out who was receiving and distributing about here. You and your helpers ought to have a reward. Who are you?" he inquired of Jim.

The boy's white teeth gleamed in a grin under his wide black mask.

" We've done you a good turn, so now you do us one by asking no questions," he replied. " We've laid the smugglers low and wiped off a score. Jolly good work, eh? Come on, chaps!" and before either coastguards or police could say another word, the smuggler-catchers vanished into the darkness, full of satisfaction that Bully Bond's days of tormenting them were done.

B. Leonard.

A CUTE CAPTURE

" You think that the Squadron Leader really will come to-night?" asked Patrol Leader Benson earnestly.

" I'm sure he will," replied the Scout Master. " Let's give him another five minutes."

The Morwell Troop had looked forward to a promised visit from Squadron Leader Beverley, whose easy, friendly and helpful manner endeared him to every one of them.

Their proudest memory was the day when the officer, dressed in his R.A.F. uniform, flying " wings " above three rows of medal ribbons, had personally conducted the troop over the aerodrome. Each scout in turn had clambered into the pilot's cockpit of a " fighter " aeroplane, and handled the flying controls. It had been a great day.

A sudden squall struck the hut of the troop, and the whistling in the roof ventilators rose to an eldritch shriek. The windows rattled like a Maxim gun. A branch of an overhanging oak tree thrummed on the iron roof.

At that moment the door flew open and a trium-

phant gust of wind rushed in, nearly extinguishing
the oil lamps before the door could be closed. A
panting R.A.F. motor-cyclist delivered his message.
The Squadron Leader was very sorry, but he was
afraid he couldn't get away. " Someone has broken
into a shed and stolen some stores," added the mes-
senger in unofficial explanation.

The faces of the expectant troop dropped.

" Never mind, chaps," said Patrol Leader Benson. " Better luck next time."

Outside the hut the troop separated.

" Come along, Whitey," called Harry Prestwood.
" Let's get on in front."

With heads bent forward against the wind, the
Patrol Leader and his Second, Dick Watts, followed
them across the fields, aiming for the red lamps
which marked the open trench of the new Morwell
water-mains.

Two of the lamps were out, and they brought
them to where Gaffer Hobbs, the night watchman,
sat over his glowing brazier.

" Drat 'em," said Gaffer, after he had relit the
lamps. " I can't keep 'em alight in this wind, and
my rheumatics——"

Dick Watts reached forward. " Let me take——"
He stopped abruptly as the wind carried to them the
sound of a long-drawn moan, dying and swelling like a
gigantic organ pipe. There was a shriek from the direction of a wood through which they would have to pass.

" What was that?" half-whispered the Patrol
Leader and Dick together.

Gaffer Hobbs withdrew his stubby pipe from his
mouth. " That be the horn of the stage coach along
what used to be the turnpike," he said with a chuckle.
" Some nights you can see the coach, with its four
greys, galloping along to the old George Inn."

At that moment, into the outer fringe of light
from the brazier, came Harry Prestwood, followed
a dozen yards behind by Whitey, his face the colour
of his flaxen hair.

Harry's teeth were rattling, and he was trembling
from hair to heel. " A g-ghost. T-there's a g-ghost
up there." He gave a quick flick with his head in the
direction of the wood.

" We were g-going along and s-suddenly a g-ghost
jumped from the side and c-came at us, dancing and
howling and screaming, a-and nearly caught us."

" Don't be an idiot," said the Patrol Leader.

" That was the coach horn—along the turnpike road," mumbled the old man. " I didn't hear the 'osses—p'raps I be getting a bit deaf."

" Come on, Dick," suggested the Patrol Leader. " I've got my torch. We'll go and see what it is, shall we?" His Second swallowed hard, but followed.

With the circle of light from the torch racing forwards and backwards in front of them, the two scouts went slowly and stealthily up the dark avenue.

For the first hundred yards they saw nothing. Another fifty yards, and still nothing. Twenty yards more and yet nothing happened.

Then, from behind an old elm stump, a white apparition seemed suddenly to blossom, and grow and grow until it reached to the branches overhead. Swirling and dancing, it came towards them.

With goggling eyes, Patrol Leader Benson and his Second stood transfixed and watched it coming. A half-strangled cry forced itself from Dick's lips as something cold and soft touched his cheek.

A soft whimper, quickly rising to a full-throated, quivering moan, filled the wood. As it died away, the white spectre ran back, and, at the last trembling quaver, seemed to vanish into the ground.

" Now, I wonder what that was?" breathed Patrol Leader Benson.

His Second tried to articulate a reply, but his lips were too dry.

The Patrol Leader flashed his torch along the hedge bordering the road. " Come on, Dick," he called, " before it has a second spasm."

He led the way through the hedge. " It's not far from here," he said confidently. " I saw——"

" Hi, m-mister!" A voice from the midst of the undergrowth brought both scouts to an abrupt halt.

" Who's that? Where are you?" called the Patrol Leader.

" O-over 'ere," came the voice rather shakily, as the eerie moan once more began to fill the wood.

At a point where the undergrowth thinned, the scouts came upon an old disused gravel hole. In it, among a number of square-looking packages, some of which had been opened and displayed their contents, crouched a man.

Almost too frightened to move, he blinked in the torchlight. " You've got me, mister—take me from this 'aunted 'ole."

Patrol Leader Benson sized up the situation in a

"Take me from this 'aunted 'ole."

flash. From the opened packages it was clear that here was the man who had broken into Squadron Leader Beverley's stores. But he looked too big a handful for two scouts to tackle.

Saying nothing, the Patrol Leader backed away a little and touched Dick on the elbow. " Dick," he whispered, " dash to the village for the police sergeant."

Dick thought of the ghost and faltered for a split second. Then he took the torch which his Patrol Leader was thrusting into his hand.

" How about you?" he whispered.

" I'll watch him until you come back," came the reply.

Dick scrambled back to the avenue, and then, with a speed that borrowed something from the howl which he heard behind him, raced to the village.

" 'Ere, what's the game?" came querulously from the craven thief. But the Patrol Leader remained silent, and began to creep back to the avenue. He was relying upon the man's fright to keep him pinned to his gravel hole until help came.

" Whr-r-oo-oo-m," came the mysterious sound,

and just then the Patrol Leader almost fell over some cords stretched taut in the undergrowth. He bent down and examined them with his fingers; then, as he slowly traced them from twisted root to root, he gave a grunt of satisfaction.

The trail took him through the hedge bordering the avenue, and as he stumbled into the ditch on the other side, something white started up from almost under him and went careering down the avenue; almost at once there came from the wood itself that prolonged " whr-r-oo-oo-m ".

The Patrol Leader waited for a moment, and in the dim light watched the " ghost's " spectral dance. As it subsided, he stumbled forward and threw himself upon it.

The thing struggled sporadically in his embrace, and once or twice almost escaped the Patrol Leader's grip. But at last, with all the wind knocked out of it, it grew inert.

With a grunt of triumph young Benson tied it up securely with the lines he had found, and left it to go in search of the accomplice in the wood.

Afterwards the Patrol Leader confessed that he could not restrain the hair on the back of his head from bristling as he stumbled through the brambles and young saplings.

Presently his toe hit something which gave a metallic ring, and he made to stoop down to examine what it was. A break in the clouds allowed a shimmering patch of moonlight to filter through the trees, and at that moment there came a shout from the avenue.

Dick had failed to find the police sergeant, but, coming across Squadron Leader Beverley, had told him the news and the officer had accompanied him back.

" Hullo, Benson," said the Squadron Leader quietly. " Where's the man?"

The Patrol Leader set out to guide him to the spot, and they had almost reached it when once again the ghostly wail rose and filled the wood with fear.

" Crumbs!" muttered the Squadron Leader as it subsided. " You've some pluck, Benson, to stay here by yourself."

The Patrol Leader glowed inwardly as they reached the gravel hole.

" This is the man all right," said the officer. " A cute capture, lads," he added smilingly.

His torch played round the undergrowth. "There's one thing missing," he announced. "A large——"

"There was another package, mister," snuffled the thief. "I opened it and a ghosty jumped out at me."

"I've got that, sir," put in the Patrol Leader, and handed to the officer a roughly tied up bundle of white silk about the size of a pillow.

"That was the ghost, Dick," he whispered, and chortled. "An airman's parachute."

"Good show, Benson," ejaculated the officer. "That bundle is worth nearly £70, and——" he broke off as the wail rose once again and drowned his voice. When it had died away, the Patrol Leader grinned. "Like to see what makes that noise, sir?"

Without waiting for a reply, Patrol Leader Benson led the party, the thief in the Squadron Leader's firm grip, to the spot where he had stubbed his toe on metal.

It was an odd freak of the wind which had caused the two elastic bands which snap open the flap of a parachute case to become stretched across the open end of one of a stack of water pipes.

A CUTE CAPTURE

Even as they looked, a gust of wind set the taut elastic twitching until the hum of its vibrations, magnified by the water pipe into a trembling moan, filled the woods for the last time.

Herbert Meredith.